This book belongs to

_____

This book is dedicated to my children - Mikey, Kobe, and Jojo.
Our anxiety doesn't come from thinking about the future, it comes from
wanting to control it.

Anxious Ninja

By Mary Nhin

Pictures by
Jelena Stupar

Anxious Ninja just needed to make it over the hill to win.
He ran and ran until he reached the finish line. 1st place!

But that was the problem. When it came to practice, no one could touch Anxious Ninja. He was the best.

But when it was time for the actual competition, his hands would get sweaty. His heart would race. And his mind kept thinking about events he couldn't control.

When his mind drifted to winning or losing, his performance would start to sink. And his anxiety would cause him to underperform.

Gritty Ninja recognized the pattern. "It's normal to feel anxiety. We all do. When I was training for the Ninja Warrior Triathlon, everyone expected me to win. And do you know what happened?" asked Gritty Ninja.

When you get anxious, just remember the 3 Rs method:

Recognize when you are thinking about situations you can't control.

Relax by taking a few slow, deep breaths.

Refocus with positive mantras like, "Everything will be okay as long as I try my best."

That weekend at the competition, Anxious Ninja lined up
with the other runners. He had one goal in mind.

His focus was at an all time high. And when the gun blasted signaling the start of the race, Anxious Ninja felt good.

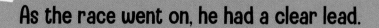

As the race went on, he had a clear lead.

But then with only two turns of the race to go, his thoughts began to shift to the finish line.

Just then, he could hear other runners catching up to him. And just like that, he lost his lead.

He needed to remember what Gritty Ninja taught him...and fast. What was it that his friend said?

He recognized and became aware of where his thoughts were.

He relaxed by taking several deep breaths.

Then, he refocused all his energy on the present and what he could control. His effort.

"Work hard," he repeated to himself. "Work hard." He sounded like a broken record, but this was his mantra. And before he knew it, he cleared the finish line...

From that day on, Anxious Ninja still experienced anxiety but the difference was now he knew how to control it, instead of letting it control him.

Sign up for new Ninja book releases at
GrowGrit.co

@marynhin   @GrowGrit
#NinjaLifeHacks

Mary Nhin   Grow Grit

Grow Grit

Made in the USA
San Bernardino, CA
21 May 2020

72151717R00018